VEGETABLE

GARDEN

Douglas Florian

Voyager Books

Harcourt Brace & Company

San Diego   New York   London

First voyager books edition 1996
Voyager Books is a registered trademark of
Harcourt Brace & Company.

Library of Congress Cataloging-in-Publication Data
Florian, Douglas.
Vegetable garden / Douglas Florian.—1st ed.
p.   cm.
"Voyager Books."
Summary: A family plants a vegetable garden and helps it grow
to a rich harvest.
ISBN 0-15-293383-2
ISBN 0-15-201018-1 pb
[1. Gardening—Fiction. 2. Vegetables—Fiction. 3. Stories in
rhyme.] I. Title.
PZ8.3F66Ve   1991
[E]—dc20   90-20620

G F

Printed in Singapore

The illustrations in this book were done in
pen and ink and watercolor on vellum paper.
The display type was set in Lithos Bold by
Thompson Type, San Diego, California.
The text type was set in Cushing Book by
Typelink, San Diego, California.
Printed and bound by Tien Wah Press, Singapore
Production supervision by Warren Wallerstein and Diana Ford
Type design by Lisa Peters

for Yonathan Lallouz

Spade, rake, hoe

Seeds in a row

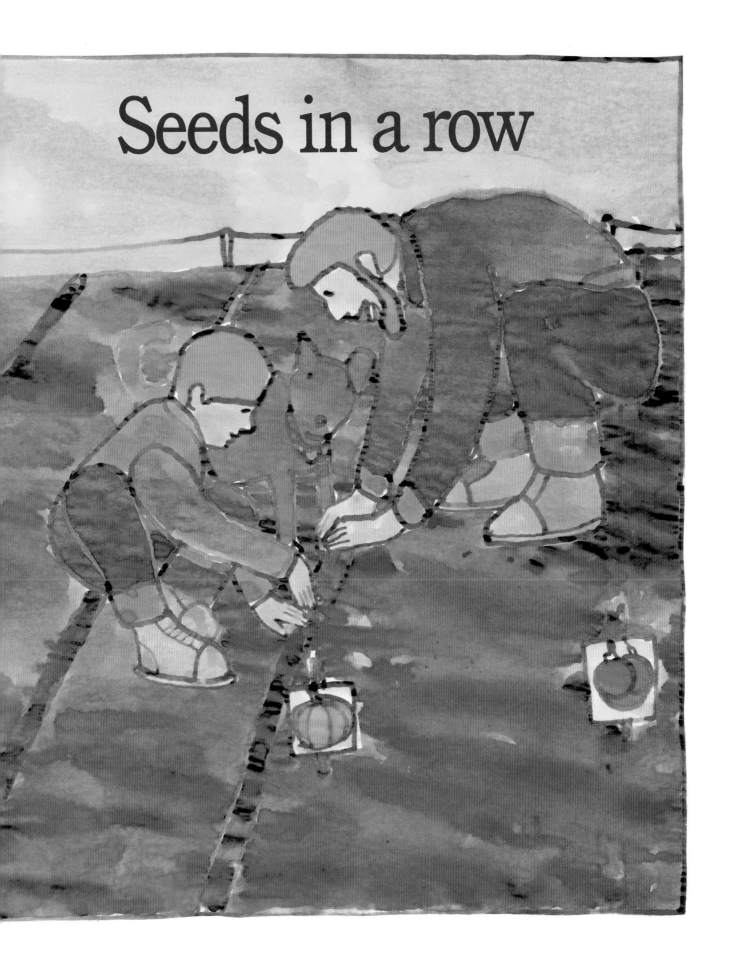

Seedlings sprout

Cucumber vine

Bright sunshine

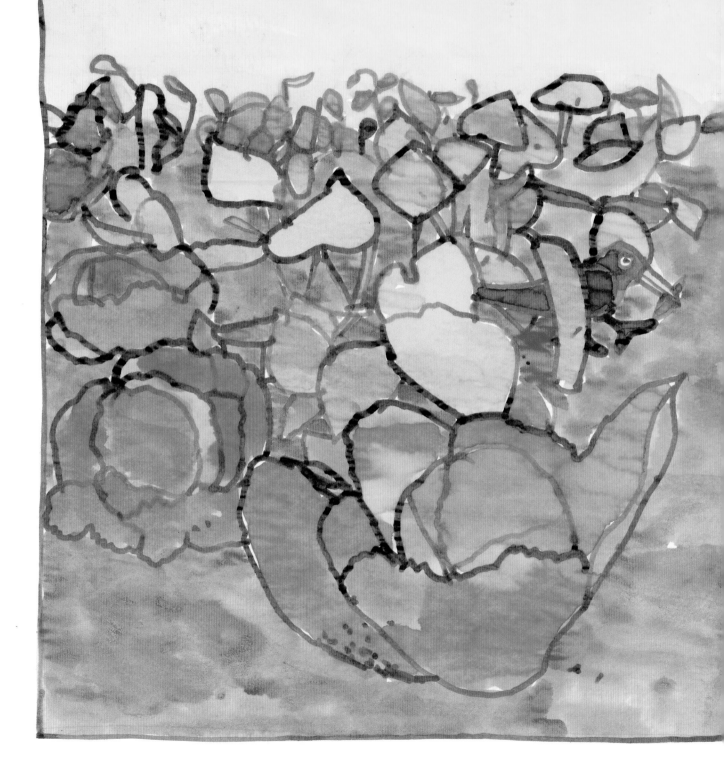

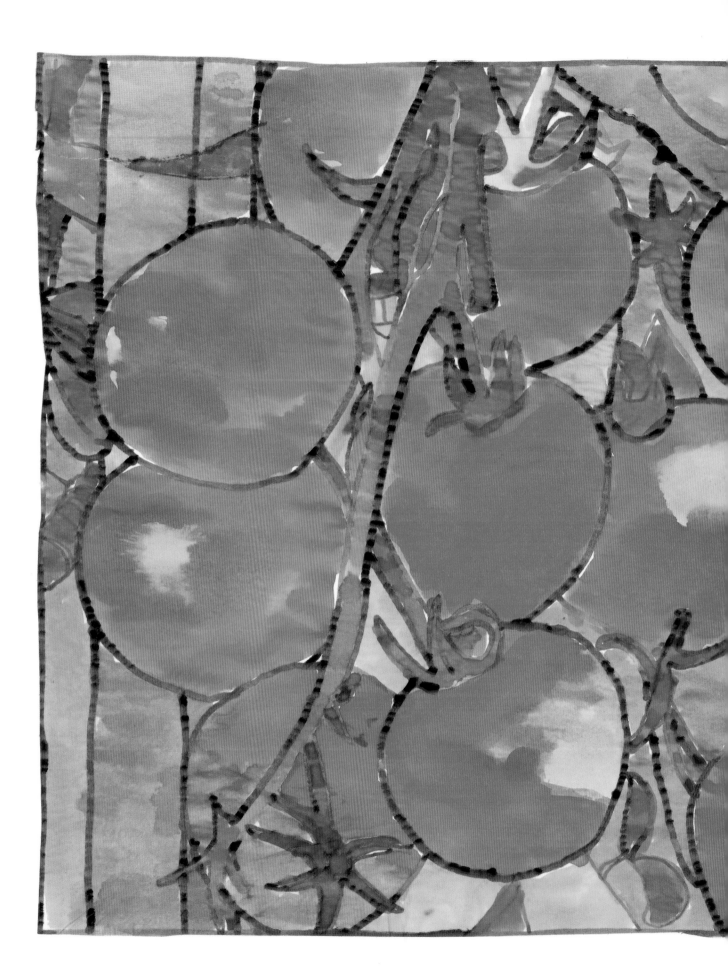

Greens and reds

Lettuce heads

Summer shower

Cauliflower

Big and round

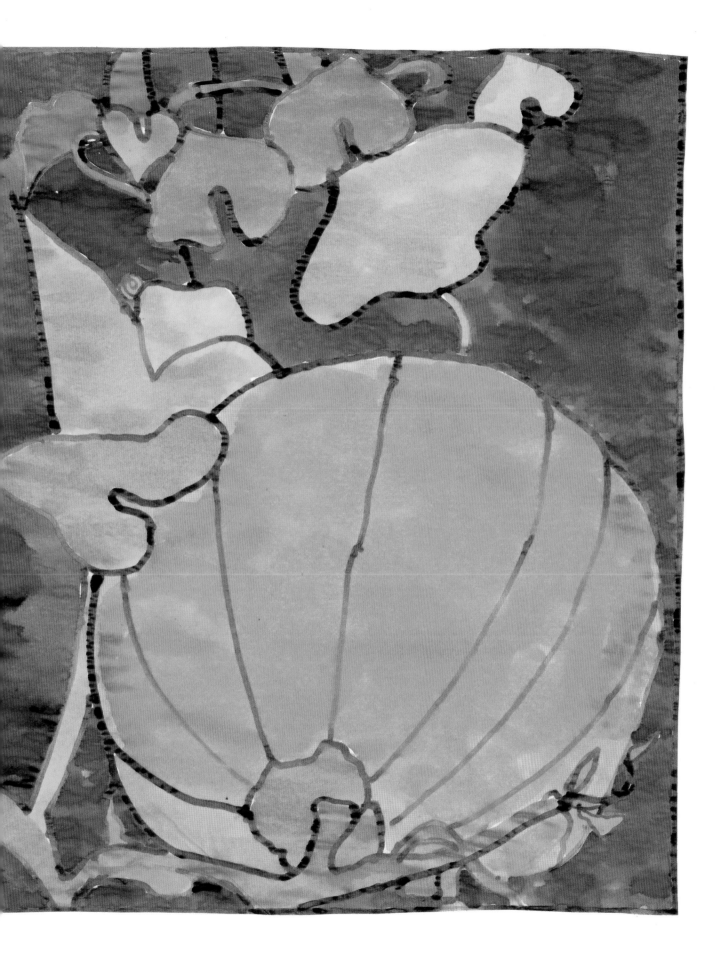

Melon mound

Pea plants climb

Harvest time